FIVE POINT FICTION

BY
RIMA

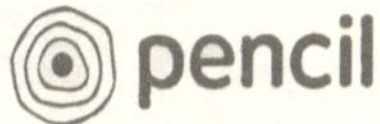
pencil

ISBN 978-93-5438-603-9
© Rima 2021
Published in India 2020 by Pencil

A brand of
One Point Six Technologies Pvt. Ltd.
123, Building J2, Shram Seva Premises,
Wadala Truck Terminal, Wadala (E)
Mumbai 400037, Maharashtra, INDIA
E connect@thepencilapp.com
W www.thepencilapp.com

DISCLAIMER: *The opinions expressed in this book are those of the authors and do not purport to reflect the views of the Publisher.*

AUTHOR BIOGRAPHY

Rima, a Software Engineer by profession, lives in Kolkata, India. A lady of thirty something years and a mother of one she enjoys reading as much as writing. Her interest spans over multiple genres though currently she is mostly focusing on Science Fiction and Fantasy. She draws her inspiration from things around her.

CONTENTS

THE FAIRIES' TALE

There was nothing to do, absolutely nothing and when you have absolutely nothing to do, you have all the time of the world in your hand, your mind is idle and you start thinking devilishly. As the saying goes - an idle mind is the devil's workshop.

The same thing happened with Flicker. He was the tiniest of the Green fairies and the youngest - just thirty-two years old which is like one-tenth of their lifespan.

What is a green fairy, you ask?

Well, they are invisible creatures, sparkling and twinkling like the stars at night. You might mistake them as the stars or the firebug in the dark. The Green fairies look like little human beings with fine wings that vibrate at a very high frequency. Their wings glow green when they vibrate, which is when they are flying. They have two antennas on their heads, protruding from their hair. Each Green fairy has antennas of different shapes and sizes. These antennas help them sense better in the dark. They have large glassy eyes and long pointy ears. They are about four inches tall, on average, from head to toe. The tallest of them had been six inches tall whom they called the giant. The smallest is Flicker who is only three inches tall. They have long fingers, but very short toes.

They live deep in the forest, invisible to human eyes, in the trees, in the bushes, in the grasses, and in the flowers. They eat fruits and drink nectar and fruit juices. They live in families, generations together. Their houses are lighted with magical embers that only they can produce. The clothes they wear are woven from leaves and grasses. Their jewelry is made from flowers.

They are ruled by the king and queen fairies, King Shamrock, and Queen Kelly-Green. The king, a fine fairy of hundred and seventy-two with darker green color, is ever ambitious and very fond of music. His queen, just ten years younger, is a beautiful fairy having a lighter green color. She is very fond of jewelry and as the flowers dry out in a few days the king has to keep in a constant supply of flowers in his palace.

No, you don't want the fairy queen to be angry.

They don't have shops or malls or supermarkets, but they have galleries and play fields and farms and gardens. They too have schools for they are an educated lot.

Our little friend, Flicker, had decided to drop school for one day. It was not the first time that he had taken this decision. He flies out of school any time he wants. That day he had decided to steal into the apple forest. He had seen someone going in there. He stopped at the gate, gave a good three sixty degrees turn and dropped straight to the ground. Two elder fairies were leisurely floating out of the gate. Flicker peeped above the little bush he was hiding behind and heaved a sigh. They were Gourmet and Dasher. Gourmet was hundred and five years old and Dasher was ninety. If they saw him hiding behind the bush they would have sent him back to school by his wings. Gourmet was almost round in the middle and very fond of juice, especially grapes. He always carried a small bottle by his waist. Dasher was more healthy and fond of fast sports. No one had been able to out-fly him so far.

Flicker waited for some time after they had left and then swiftly flew inside. The orchard was huge having a hundred trees and he had to find his quarry in it. All he had seen was a red streak, but he knew he was not wrong.

It was her.

Her name was Scarlet. She was only twenty-five years old; two and a half inches tall and the most sparkly of her kind. She had long red hair touching her feet, long round wings like water drops and large and brown eyes. Her antennae were like two balls that nodded in every direction like balls on a spring. She was beautiful, Flicker thought, but he had never been able to talk to her. It was not their language since they had a common tongue. It was not that they didn't know each other for they knew each other very well but the reason that Flicker couldn't speak to her was that she was a Red.

The Red fairies were just like the Green fairies only that their color was red instead of green.

The Red fairies didn't come inside the territory of the Green fairies and the Green fairies didn't go anywhere near the Red Kingdom. They were not to speak to each other under any circumstances.

There are many laws that the fairies, both Red and Green, follow, bend and break, but there was one law, mother of all laws as it was called, that no fairy would ever dare to break. If any fairy was found guilty of violating the mother law, then he or she would be banished from the kingdom. They are taught about the rules at schools from a very young age. They are made to understand the importance of a regulation, its necessity and of the penalty that would be inflicted on them if they tend to break any of them.

Almost twenty Green fairies and fifteen Red fairies had been banished in a span of three hundred years.

Flicker, being just a kid, knew of the rule. His mother, like every other mother, had warned him of the danger in talking to a Red fairy. You shouldn't even look at one, she had said. But what Flicker couldn't understand was why he should not talk to a beautiful fairy like Scarlet. The Red fairies sparkle all over. Their wings don't glow.

He flew on top of the tree and hid behind an apple. From there he could see Scarlet flitting from tree to tree. She looked from one apple to another looking for something specific. Then she stopped at one point, near an apple almost as red as herself and as large as herself. She looked around her and then pulled it by hugging it with both her hands. She couldn't even reach her other hand on the other side. Her wings flapped at high speed pulling the branch down, but the apple didn't break from the branch. Then suddenly her hands slipped. The branch sprang upwards and Scarlet, owing to the potential she had gained, was tossed backward. She went into the branches of the tree behind her and fell through it. Flicker could distinctly hear the twigs breaking. Scarlet landed on the soft grass below. She lay still. Flicker wasn't the only one to hear the breaking of twigs. BarrelTop, the keeper of the orchard, had heard it too. He came rushing to the tree. Flicker quickly flew down and covered Scarlet with the biggest leaf he could find and then lay on top of it, massaging his head.

BarrelTop looked at the mess and frowned at Flicker.

"You were supposed to be in school, Flikei," he said. He had a heavy voice. His antennae were shaped like barrels giving him the name. He was eighty years old and very pale green in color. "What are you doing here?"

"Came for my lunch," Flicker said. "Can I please have that apple?"

He pointed at the one Scarlet had been trying to break. BarrelTop shook his head and flew up for it. Taking the chance Flicker peeped under the leaf. Scarlet was stirring, but her eyes were still closed. Flicker dropped the leaf as BarrelTop came down with two apples.

"Here," he tossed them towards Flicker and then nodded towards the gate. "Go back to school."

Flicker nodded and BarrelTop went away. Flicker picked up the leaf and whispered, "Are you alright?"

Scarlet nodded. Flicker extended the apples. Scarlet, at first scared of this Green fairy, didn't even try to stand up. Flicker looked right and left and went under the leaf. Scarlet crouched even further.

"Don't be scared," Flicker said. "Take this before he comes back."

Scarlet stretched her hand and quickly took away the apple. She murmured a thank you too. Flicker stepped back from under the leaf. A second later Scarlet stepped out. She was shy and looked down at her feet. She was wearing a tunic made from pink lotus having a belt made from a blade of wild grass.

"Go," Flicker urged. He was scared that they would be discovered. Scarlet, her cheeks were cherry red now, took one or two steps and then shot up and almost disappeared.

Somewhere deep in the forest, on the other side of the narrow, dusty pathway, was sitting a Red fairy, with a bamboo flute in his hand, his eyes looking up into the night sky. He went by the name of Piccolo. He was looking at Orion, the hunter. There was a light breeze that night. The trees were murmuring among themselves. The sky was clear, the moon was high and Piccolo started to hum. He had a sweet voice, musical and full of soul.

The moon is rising high,

In the night sky,

The stars shine bright,

With all their might.

Tomorrow it will be,

Another day to see,

For you and me darling,

Just for you and me.

He hummed the lines a few times and then touched the flute with his wet red lips and blew into the hole. A sweet soul touching tune floated along with the wind spreading far and wide into the forest. Slowly and gently it melted into the night air, becoming one with the forest.

The Red fairy king, King Ritzy, was sitting by the window of his palace tree and reading a book. Ritzy put down the book and looked up. The music of the night came in through the window. Ritzy is a tall, four inches, and broad fairy of exactly a hundred years. He is dark red in color and quick with swords. He loves to read books and listen to music.

"Isn't it beautiful?" His queen, Queen Folly, said. She is a beautiful young fairy of ninety-five. She was combing her red hair near the mirror then. "Can we go on vacation?" She asked.

"No dear," Ritzy said. "The centipedes are crawling all around the pear gardens. We have to drive them out."

The Red fairies are a fighting lot. They make strategies, create new weapons, plan their defenses but never attack. The Green fairies are more peace-loving and they tend to talk out of situations while the Reds let their swords do the talking.

The centipedes were enemies of both fairies. They are ghastly creatures crawling in the mud. They eat away the fruits and trees and destroy all the food.

While the Green fairies had made a deal with them the Red fairies had decided to drive them away.

The queen shuddered. "So many fairies will die," she said.

The scales of the centipedes are stronger than the weapons the fairies had and to harm or kill a centipede they had to go under them.

Ritzy was well aware of this, but there was no other way.

"Can't we make a deal with them as the Greens did?" Folly asked. Ritzy stood up from his chair and floated lightly towards his queen.

"No," he said in a heavy voice. "We can't. We will…"

There was someone at the door.

"Who is it?" Ritzy turned his head.

The curtains parted and a little Red fairy walked in.

"Hello father," she said. "Hello, mother."

"Scarlet?" Her mother said. "Come in dear."

Scarlet came in. "Dinner is ready," she announced.

On the farther side of the Red Kingdom, even further from the Green, resided the centipedes. They were thousands in number and ruthless killers. They ate fairies for breakfast. Their king, Killipide, was the longest of them all. He ate roaches for dinner and ate more than one at a time. These centipedes destroyed the gardens and farms that the fairies had. They are not afraid of anything except… well, everyone is afraid of it. It was fire.

About a thousand years ago when the Red and Green fairies used to live together – oh, yes there was such a time – these were not so many in number. There had always been wars between the centipedes and the fairies. On one such war, when the centipedes were almost victorious, one of the Red fairy soldiers cut down the head of the then centipede king with the help of a Green fairy soldier.

At the end of the battle, after the remaining centipedes were driven out and peace was restored, it was time for honoring the heroes. But the then king, a Green fairy, Glum-Ore, had something else in mind. He honored the Green fairies only and not the Red ones. This hurt the sentiments of the Red fairies and they protested, peacefully. Glum-ore ordered his soldiers to force out any protesters by any means. In the process, many of the Red fairies got injured. The Reds, thus disrespected and insulted, separated from the Greens and had remained separated ever since.

The Red fairies had always been brave and courageous and ready for war. The Greens, however, are a bit laid back and lethargic. They are more of artistic mind and cultural. Just like Palette, a Green fairy of one fifty is an artist. He sat on his settee by the window with a plate of colors in his left hand, a paintbrush in his right hand and white blank canvas in front of him. His eyes were on the sky, his mind even further away.

There are few fairies, both Red and Green, who can perform magic. These fairies are called Gremlins. They are said to be blessed with the rare gift of nature and they tend to the king and queen and help in ruling the kingdom. It was this magic that had kept the centipedes away. Both the fairies had put up a magic wall around their kingdom that had helped them to detect any unwanted entries.

That day a gremlin going by the name of Four-Finger – for he had only four fingers in his left hand – had detected Scarlet coming into the Green Kingdom. Four-Finger was soft at heart. He had seen Scarlet come and go before but he had not reported. She is merely an infant and how could he see her banished? But that day when Scarlet was leaving another gremlin, Pulsar, had seen her too. Pulsar was good at heart but very strict with rules. He was also Flicker's grandfather.

The Gremlins have their Headquarters on the tree beside the palace tree. There are seven Green Gremlins who have magical powers. They are called the supreme. There are other fairies with magical powers too and they are called Pixies. Pixies have less magical power and they help the gremlins in performing their tasks.

When Pulsar entered the chamber, Four-Finger was teaching two pixies how to create fire by snapping one's thumb and forefinger.

"Pixies," Pulsar called gently. He has a heavy voice. He is the head of the Gremlins. He is five inches tall and has a silver beard. The three fairies looked up and then stood up. "Kindly wait outside the chamber."

The two pixies bowed and left the chamber. Pulsar put down the scrolls he was carrying and turned to Four-Finger.

"Well, Four-Finger," he smiled. "How was the day?"

"It's good, Pulsar," Four-Finger said.

"Haven't seen any Reds around, have we?"

Four-Finger swallowed.

Pulsar sat down on his chair at the head of the table.

"Sit," he said. Four-Finger sat down. "It was that little red one, wasn't it?"

Four-Finger nodded.

"Scarlet," he said, "isn't it?"

Four-Finger nodded again.

"What are you going to do?"

"She is just a little kid," Four-Finger murmured.

"I know," Pulsar patted his hand, knowing how soft-hearted Four-Finger was. "But it's important that she learns the rules at a young age."

Four-Finger made to rise, but Pulsar waved him to sit. "I'll talk to the majesty."

Flicker was waiting at the dining table when Pulsar came in. Flicker being the youngest was his grandfather's favorite. He flew up from his seat and hugged Pulsar from behind.

"Caught you, grandpa," he giggled. "Caught you again."

"Yes, sonny, you caught me again," Pulsar patted his head and smiled. He made a circle in the air and tapped it on the top. A ball dropped down on to the floor. "There you go."

Flicker picked up the ball and flew out the window. He loved his grandpa's magic balls. When you throw them towards the sky, they go high in the air, keep afloat there for some time glowing like a fireball and then burst open like a firecracker sprinkling shards of various shapes and colors all over the forest. Flicker liked to catch them as the fell.

The forest was quiet and asleep. Flicker came out till the Great Tree. The Great Tree, a banyan, is the oldest of all trees and is right at the center of the forest. It's equidistance from both the kingdoms and belongs to no one. This tree is home to hundreds of birds. They are all Flicker's friends.

He flew to the top the Great Tree, looked around and threw the ball as hard as he could towards the sky. The ball zoomed up about miles in the air before it stopped. It glowed like the moon. Then it burst. As it burst it lighted the forest like the day. Flicker dashed for the first flake but stopped midway. The flake landed on his head and then disappeared. But Flicker didn't notice that. His eyes had fallen on a little sparkly thing behind a leaf of the banyan tree. It was shivering. Very carefully

Flicker came down to it and even more carefully he lifted the leaf.

There she was: The little Red fairy of the Red Kingdom.

"Scarlet!" the name slipped out of Flicker's lips. He quickly covered his mouth and hid behind the leaf himself. Scarlet, on her part, startled looking up and drew the leaf towards herself.

"What do you want?" she asked, wiping her tears.

Flicker peeped round the edge of the leaf. "Why are you here?"

Scarlet sniffed a little bit and wiped her nose. "Your grandfather had seen me come to the apple orchard yesterday. He informed my father and I am banished," she explained and started to cry again.

Flicker lowered the leaf and stood on the twig, his head hanging low. He was very fond of this little fairy. As he saw her cry he felt like crying himself.

"Don't cry, Scarlet," he said slowly. "See, this is a no-fairy land. It doesn't belong to the Reds or the Greens." He said trying to sound as confident as he could. "You can stay here."

"I am scared," Scarlet confessed.

Flicker was sacred himself. But then he knew someone. His name was Red-Tail for he had a red spot on his tail. He was a sparrow living in a tree just two trees away from the Great Tree.

"Come with me," Flicker said and flew off. Scarlet, not understanding what Flicker meant, followed him slowly.

Red-Tail was home having dinner with his wife Flare. They were just discussing how long the warms were that Flare had been able to dig up when Flicker came calling at their nest.

"Hope I am not interrupting," he said and curtsied. Red-Tail was more than pleased to see him. He flew out of his nest followed by his wife.

"Flicker Fairy," he said spreading his wings. "What's brings…" his eyes had fallen on Scarlet. "What is a Red doing with you?"

Flicker narrated his story and Flare shook her head. "Poor kid. So she has no home to stay?"

Flicker and Scarlet shook their heads. Flicker asked, "Can she stay with you?"

"He banished her?" This was the fourth time that Four-Finger asked the same question. "His own daughter? She is just a kid."

Pulsar nodded but said nothing. He had not expected Ritzy to banish his own only twenty-five years old daughter. The news had spread all over the fairy kingdom. Some said it was a right thing to do for a righteous king. Some said it was cruel to banish a little fairy of twenty-five. She was barely an infant.

Flicker's mother, CarPoly, a very dark Green fairy, was worried to her wings. She was sure the Green king would banish Flicker too. But Flicker was not worried about that. He knew Scarlet would be safe and she was in No-Fairy Land he could meet her whenever he wanted.

As days went by Scarlet and Flicker became friends. They met at night, spoke about their lives in their respective kingdoms, Flicker even told Scarlet all that he learned at school. The sparrows didn't mind having them in their nest. They made friends with other birds like the Jacobin cuckoo going by the name of Coots and a white-browed coucal calling himself Karl. The snowy owl named Hooter and the elf owl named Picket were their every night's company. The ruby topaz hums around them whenever they were flying together deep in conversation. She calls herself Ruby and is a constant hummer. About a mile north of the Great Tree was a lake. It is called the Lake of Souls. Its water remains as still as a mirror and just like a mirror you can see your reflection in its water.

Every night Scarlet and Flicker used to fly to the lake. There they met the great hornbill. He was a kingfisher and his name was Yellow-Beak. There they met the pair of white swans, Cyngus and his wife Cyngini. They are always seen together. There was a black swan too. He is called Lustre because of the glaze his feathers throw off.

With time the two fairies became very fond of each other. They found so much common in them that they began to wonder what could have kept the Greens and the Reds separated for so long. On the nights when Flicker could not come Scarlet used to sit by the Lake all by herself and listen to the stories, the swans had to tell.

On one such night when Flicker had not come, Scarlet was sitting alone by the lake. Cyngus and Cyngini were not there yet. Lustre had just swum by her wishing her a good evening.

The water was still like a mirror and the night sky was recreated in its reflection. She could almost count the stars. Once or twice the stillness was broken as the wind made tiny ripples on the surface. Scarlet was searching for the constellations she had read in school and the ones Flicker had shown her when a star broke and fell. Scarlet flew up and looked around. The forest was quietly sleeping. The night owls were wooing somewhere in the west, the crickets were chirping merrily. She could even distinguish Cypher, the long-tailed cricket of the Green Kingdom. He chirped the loudest and always had a different rhythm altogether.

She could even hear Piccolo sing the night song and Banjo, the pale green fairy playing his mandolin in his own tune.

Then something flew by her. She whirled around but there was no one.

"Flikei?" She called. "Is that you?"

Only the wind tapped the leaves on the trees. Something whizzed past her.

"Flicker?" She called again. "Please don't scare me like that."

Something flapped over her head and a leaf dropped down. Scarlet wrapped herself in her arms and flew towards the tree.

The big tree, with hardly any leaves, its branches sprawling in every direction, looked ghostly. It was very dark that night, a new moon night. Both the kingdoms would celebrate the night in an hour. Maybe that was why Flicker hadn't come.

Scarlet looked around her and shivered.

"Hello? Is anyone..."

"She is a fairy," a voice said. It was husky and very dry.

"Does she have blood?" Another grumbling voice said. Scarlet turned this way and that but could not see anyone. She, very slowly, started to come down but then two eyes opened in front of her. They were red and cruel. Scarlet turned and dived but something caught her and pressed her against the branch.

"A Red fairy!" It said. Scarlet let out a scream on seeing the pair of canines shining behind its lips. It was a bat, a vampire bat.

He flapped his wings and made a strange sound. Immediately, five more bats appeared behind him.

"What have you got, Canny?" one of them asked.

The one bat called Canny, he was the one holding Scarlet, smiled. "A Red fairy. We will…"

He couldn't finish his statement. Something hit him and pushed him against the tree. The other bats were so stunned that they looked at each other and then at Canny and his attacker.

"Fly away," a thin strained voice said. Scarlet startled on hearing Flicker's voice.

"Flicker?" she could barely see him behind those black wings of the bat.

The other bats looked about themselves and the moment Scarlet spoke they grabbed her from all sides. Then something hit one of them on the head and he fell down. The others looked about themselves but saw nothing. Then another bat was hit by something flying, but couldn't see anything. They were now scared. They let go of Scarlet and flapped away in any direction they could. Then Scarlet saw Hooter fly down and grab Canny by his claws and threw him away from the groove where he was trying to strangle Flicker. He looked carefully downwards and then turned.

"Get him," he said. "He is here."

Two fairies, one Green and one Red, came down and gently lifted Flicker in their arms and carried him out of the groove.

It was a big tree, a full grown maple tree, almost golden in the autumn. Deep inside its branches were grooves where the fairies lived. There were Green fairies and Red fairies living together and Scarlet looked at them with awe. She was sitting beside the bed where Flicker was lying. He was asleep. There were scratches on his arms but he was otherwise alright. An elderly Red fairy lady was attending to his injuries. Her name was Raspberry for her antennas looked like raspberries. There was a Green fairy named Chi. He was young, only eighty, and was a pixie. Behind him was an elderly Green fairy with long silver bread and even longer hair. His ears were pointy and his antennas were perfect spheres. He was called Elixir. He was two hundred years old and was a potion brewing fairy. At that moment he was brewing a potion for Flicker.

There were other fairies too. Scarlet could see them peeping through the windows. Then she saw Ruby. She hummed into the room and perched on the chair.

"How is he?" she asked.

Raspberry smiled gently. "He will be fine by morning. He is a tough fairy. He is our Flikei."

Scarlet looked amazed.

"You know him?" she asked.

"We know you too, young princess," Chi said and bowed.

Scarlet looked all around her. "Do you stay here? Together?"

"Yes," Chi said. "We were all banished and we came here."

Ritzy stood by the window and looked at the stars. In a minute the celebration would begin. Everyone would be celebrating with fireworks and crackers. Everyone would be smiling and cheering and enjoying with their families and he would join them as their king but he wouldn't be enjoying. He knew he would laugh but not be happy. He would light the first lantern that was hung at door but there wouldn't be any light that night. How could there be when his dear little girl wasn't there?

The door opened and his queen came in. She had cried for so long that her eyes seemed to have lost their brightness. Ritzy turned to her and sighed.

"I am sorry, Folly," he said. "But..."

Folly forced a smiled and wiped a tear that had appeared so suddenly. "I understand. It's time."

Hand in hand they came out of their tree. There would be a crowd of fairies. The king would light the first lantern and one by one everyone would light their lanterns and take them home. But that night there were none. Ritzy and Folly stood in front of the crowd that had gathered at their doorsteps empty-handed. There was no smiling or laughing or cheering. There were only sad faces and misty eyes that looked at their king with sadness and compassion. Ritzy lighted the lantern. For minutes he looked at it and then turned and slowly went inside. Folly watched the little fire for some time longer, wiped another tear and went away. One by one, the other fairies, their head hanging low, left the palace tree. The door to the palace tree closed and the new moon night was dark once again. Only one tiny dot of light flickered in that darkness. Piccolo blew into his flute again.

No moon in the sky,

No stars to watch.

No light to look at,

It's a dim dark world.

No song to sing tonight,

No song to praise.

None, my dear princess,

None, my lost grace.

Presto, the sentry fairy of the Green kingdom was flying high that night. He watched the whole incident from the top and dashed towards the Green fairy palace tree. Shamrock was waiting for him. Presto bowed and narrated the whole incident.

"It's awful," Kelly-Green said.

"Tell everyone," Shamrock said, "that we are not celebrating this new moon night. If anyone wants to hang a lantern he might."

Presto bowed and zapped away again. He zipped and zapped from one place to another and that was why he got the name Presto.

That night there was no lantern lit in the Green kingdom either.

Four-Finger sighed standing by the window. "I feel terrible, Pulsar. I feel responsible."

Pulsar nodded absentmindedly. He had his mind set on other things. Flicker had not returned yet and he couldn't trace him. He knew that Flicker went away somewhere every night and he came back before midnight but that night he hadn't. Pulsar was hovering up and down the room when a pixie flew in, his wings almost falling off.

"Danger," he said and panted.

Pulsar and Four-Finger caught him and sat him down. Four-Finger gave him some juice to drink.

"What danger?" Pulsar asked.

"Centipedes," the pixie said. "They are approaching the Lake of Souls."

Both the Gremlins startled at the news. Pulsar asked: "how many?"

"Thousands," the pixie said. "They look horrible."

Pulsar flew off.

King Shamrock and Queen Kelly-Green were sitting on a leaf outside their bedroom and counting the stars when a guard fairy asked for permission to come in.

"Gremlin Pulsar wishes to meet the king, your highness."

Shamrock looked up at the sky. It was long past midnight. Why would Pulsar want to meet him then? He nodded at the guard and told him to ask Pulsar to wait at the hall.

Pulsar was again hovering to and fro in the hall when Shamrock came in. Pulsar bowed to the king.

"The centipedes are approaching the Lake of Souls, sire," he said without any preamble.

Shamrock, taken aback by the sudden news, startled and then frowned. "Are you sure Pulsar?"

"Yes," the Gremlin nodded. "I am sure. And if they are approaching the Lake of Souls then the bats will be with them."

Shamrock didn't need to be reminded of that. He thought only for a moment and then called in a guard.

Flicker sat up on the bed and scratched his head. He looked around and found Scarlet sitting by him. She was smiling but there were tears in her eyes.

"Scarlet?" Flicker asked. "Are you alright?"

The little fairy nodded. "Thank you, Flicker. You saved my life."

Flicker smiled broadly and sprang up from the bed. "Let's go and see the celebration."

Elixir came in at that moment. He saw Flicker and smiled.

"So," he came near. "Our little Flikei is up and flying again."

"Yes," Flicker nodded bobbing his two antennas. "We are going to see the celebration."

Elixir smiled tenderly. "There is no celebration, my dear."

Scarlet and Flicker looked at each other and then they both startled as a noise came from outside. It was Hooter and he was wooing as loudly as he could. Beside him was Ruby and she was flapping so hard that her wings almost vanished. Elixir came out and looked about.

"What is it Hooter?" he asked. "You scared the wings off my back."

Hooter came down and perched on a branch. "The bats are circling on the other side of the Lake. The centipedes must be nearby."

The three fairies could feel their skin crawling. Scarlet grabbed Flicker's arm. Flicker swallowed hard. Elixir flew straight up as high as he could and stopped when he could see the other side of the Lake. The forest was swathed in a blanket of darkness. The Green kingdom was on his right and the Red was on his left. At the center there was the Great Tree and down to the north was the Lake of Souls. Beyond the Lake was the Dead Forest of the centipedes. He could see the bats circling the entrance of the Dead Forest.

Slowly he came down. By that time others have gathered there too.

"What is it Elixir?" Raspberry asked.

"The bats are circling," he said. "The centipedes are coming."

"What are we going to do?" Raspberry's voice choked.

"We can't fight," Chi squeaked.

"We need to warn the kingdoms," Scarlet said. She was scared but her voice was steady. Flicker came forth.

"I can warn the Greens," he said. "And the Reds."

"They are coming closer," Coots came flapping his wings. "They are on the other side of the Lake. The bats are ready to carry them across."

"We are doomed," Ruby dropped on the branch next to Hooter.

Picket flew in. "I see a fairy go into the Red Kingdom. It's Dasher."

Everyone looked at the other.

Suddenly the coucal, Karl, yelled and flew away. Something dropped from the sky. Everyone looked up and found the bats dropping the centipedes one after the other. Everyone flew away in any direction they could. Flicker caught Scarlet and dashed for the sparrows' nest. He shoved her inside.

"You will be safe in here," he said.

"What do you mean?" Scarlet turned around. "Where are you going?"

"Well someone needs to make sure they don't get into the kingdoms." Flicker shrugged.

Scarlet caught hold of his hand. "But we are just kids. What can we do?"

Flicker scratched his head. "I don't know. But if we can warn the kingdoms they can at least protect themselves," he said and then added doubtfully, "I hope."

The bats dropped the centipedes near the Lake and flew away to bring more. Lustre watched them come and go. He hated the bats but he hated the centipedes more. He looked back and found Cyngus and Cyngini.

"Well?" he asked. "Do we sit here with our wings clapped?"

Cyngus was looking at the warms as they crawled on the ground. "No," he said. "We will fight back but right now we can't do anything. We need the fairies' magic."

Lustre nodded and turned back to the bank. The centipedes had grown in number.

Yellow-Beak, the kingfisher made himself available on the tree closest to the Lake and started counting the numbers. Picket and Hooter started to circle the Lake. The centipede paid no attention. They crawled their way towards the Great Tree. Suddenly a streak of green light shot across the sky. Everyone – the owls, the kingfisher, the banished Red and Green fairies, the sparrows, the swans, even the bats, and the centipedes – looked up at the sky. The green streaks of light showed again and then again and then again.

The centipedes raised their heads to see and saw the Green warrior fairies flying in circles. Out of the circle came Viridian. He was a Gremlin, like Pulsar. He floated downwards gradually and then settled a foot above the first centipede.

"I would like to speak with your King," he said. He was the Green kingdom's spokesman.

The centipede that Viridian addressed growled and turned to speak. After a while, a big, fat and large centipede approached. The other centipedes moved aside to make space for him.

"What do you want?" he asked in a rumbling kind of voice.

Viridian held his head high. "Killipide," he spoke. "I, on behalf of his highness, Shamrock, want to remind you that we had a deal. We paid you fifty apples and a hundred oranges this full moon night. And besides, you can't tread on this land."

Killipide spat on the soil and grinned.

"Tell your Shamrock that we had a change of mind. From now on we only have fairies on our menu."

He said and all the centipedes started laughing. Flicker could feel his bones shivering.

Viridian listened quietly for some time and then nodded. "Very well," he said and zoomed up. No sooner did he do so hundreds of green flashes hailed down from the sky.

A few centipedes that were not ready got caught in the green flames and turned and twisted. Others coiled themselves into their shells.

The centipedes were more prepared this time. They drew out their spikes and started firing at the fairies. A few fairies, who were not expecting a counterattack, got caught in them and fell down to the ground.

"I can't watch this," Scarlet said and hid her face.

"Can't we do something?" Flicker asked Elixir. "You are a Gremlin."

There were flashes of green lights as the Green fairies flew in and out of the centipedes' cluster trying to kill them. Yellow-Beak was picking up as many centipedes as he could and dropped them into Lake drowning them forever. But that was not enough.

"I don't care what happens," Picket said. "I am going to smash these centies for good tonight."

"Don't be in a haste my friend," Elixir said. "They are more in number. Look."

They looked the way Elixir pointed and saw more and more centipedes being carried across the lake.

"Can't we stop them from coming?" Flicker said.

"We can't," Raspberry said. "Cyngus, Cyngini and Lustre can stop them."

"Then why aren't they?" Scarlet pleaded.

"Because they need our magic," Chi said. He had just flown down from the top branch. "They need the combined magic from both the Red and Green fairies and only then they can stop the centipedes. The creepers are gaining on the fairies."

"I don't care," Flicker said. "I don't care what the law says but I am going to fight."

"And how are you going to do that?" Hooter asked.

The cries from the battle below were blood-chilling.

Flicker looked at the battle below and then dived but he didn't go far. Something caught him from behind and stopped him from flying any farther. He found himself surrounded in a red ball. Everyone turned around and found the Red king Ritzy floating a little above with his minister, Cerise. Cerise was a Gremlin and it was he who was holding Flicker.

"You, my little fairy," Ritzy said, "are going nowhere."

Everyone after having swallowed the fact that the Red King was actually there, bowed. Elixir came forward and bowed. "Sire, we are honored to have you here."

"The honor is mine Elixir to see you again. Now if you would excuse me," he said and made to go when a green glow descended from above.

Shamrock came down followed by Pulsar.

"I wished it was a happy new moon night, Ritzy," the Green king said.

"I wish the same," Ritzy said and turned to Cerise. "Well, you know what to do."

With that word, Pulsar and Cerise flew up towards the Lake.

The battle was raging on with the centipedes killing more fairies by the minute. Flicker flew up to see and found more centipedes being dropped by the bats. But what caught his eyes was Pulsar and Cerise circling over the lake and the swan couple and Lustre sitting at the center stretching their necks upwards.

Scarlet flew up beside Flicker.

"Look over there, Flikei," she pointed at the other end of the Lake. "The bats just keep on coming."

"Scarlet," Flicker said scratching his head. "If we can stop the bats, we can stop the centipedes from coming."

"But how?"

"Bats hate lights," Coots said from behind.

"But it's the dead of night," Scarlet said and rubbed her hands in distress. Suddenly sparks flew out of them.

Both Flicker and Coots looked surprisingly at her. "How did you do that?" Coots asked.

Scarlet had no idea. She rubbed her palms again and again sparks flew out of them.

"Wait," Flicker said. "Clap. Clap very hard."

Scarlet struck her palms together as hard as she could and lightning flashed from them.

"Perfect, Scarlet," Flicker hugged her. "You are a Pixie. I have an idea."

Flicker flew back to the tree where others were. There he shared his idea.

"Grab a branch everybody," Hooter said. "A twig for you Ruby."

Karl flew above everyone with a long branch and yelled at the top of his voice. "Let's get this done with. The featherless bats will learn never to cross the Lake after this."

They flew across the lake where Scarlet was waiting with Coots.

"Alright, Scarlet," Flicker said. "Light them all up."

One by one Scarlet lighted the branches. Little by little there was light. More birds from the Great Tree came to join. As the number grew it became brighter.

"Let's drive the bats out of here," Picket screamed and they flew towards the other side of the Lake, together. Seeing the lights the bats started to flee dropping the centipedes wherever they could.

Scarlet and Flicker were more than happy. They went round and round holding their hands in happiness before something snatched Flicker away and buried him into the bark of a thorny tree.

It was Canny.

He was angry that the other bats had fallen prey to the birds and were fleeing away. He clawed Flicker by his neck and bared his canines.

"You will die tonight, little fairy," he said. Flicker closed his eyes in fear.

"Let him go," Scarlet yelled from behind. She was not scared. Canny turned to see her and laughed. He closed his grip on Flicker's throat. The little Green fairy almost fainted. But Scarlet was ready. She clapped her hand so hard that the flash of lightning cut across the air casting Canny away from the tree and into the Lake. The lightning had pushed away Scarlet as well. She hadn't learned to brace herself yet. She hit something and looked up to find Chi holding her from behind. Elixir brought Flicker up in his arms.

"You two are very brave," he smiled. "But these bats and centipedes are stronger."

"Look," Chi said pointing at the Lake. It was a sight to watch.

After the bats had retreated the centipedes were falling short in numbers. No matter how much they curled up the fairies, both Red and Green found one or the other way to hurt them.

Then came their nightmare.

Cyngus, Cyngini, and Lustre spread their wings over the Lake of Souls. Their wings covered almost the half of the lake. Then they flew over the forest and came circling down towards the battle. The fairies left the centipedes alone and dashed off. And the centipedes started crawling in every direction they could. But there was no escape for them. At first, Cyngus folded his wings behind him and came down in a headlong dive. Just above the battlefield he abruptly spread his wings creating a shockwave. It flattened the centipedes, even blew away some of them, disarming them at the same time. The king, Killipide, raised his fang and screamed.

"This is unfair," he cried. "This is unrighteous."

"No," Lustre said from above. "This is justice."

He spread his wings wide. His feathers were like on silvery fire. They glowed so bright that it seemed like a hundred moons were shining together amidst the forest. He blazed and clapped his wings forming a flash that swept over the centipedes burning them. After the light subdued there was no sign of the centipedes left. Only the wounded and injured fairies were seen lying on the ground. Cyngini came down slowly and spread her wings over them showering them with a soft glow. One by one the fairies woke up and then stood up, their wounds healed completely.

The battle was won. The centipedes were defeated.

Pulsar and Cerise returned with Ritzy and Shamrock behind them. Ritzy was leaning over Shamrock for he had hurt his left wing. Raspberry swiftly flew over to the king. Ritzy smiled softly as the Red fairy attended to his wound.

Viridian glanced at Shamrock and, as the latter nodded, flew up to hover above everyone.

"Tonight, on a new moon night, we have defeated the centipedes," he said. "We the fairies, not the Greens or the Reds but the fairies," he said and bowed. "By His Majesty's wish, we, the Greens, offer our hands to the Reds in friendship."

All the fairies looked at each other.

Shamrock looked up. "Well Ritzy," he said. "I think we have done enough damage already. It's time that we unite. Only then we can survive."

Ritzy glanced at Cerise and then at Elixir. They both nodded. He turned towards his daughter being comforted by Chi and smiled.

"Shamrock," he said. "The doors at Red kingdom are already open."

Well, folks there you have it. Ever since then the Red and the Green fairies have lived like friends. The mother of all laws was dissolved. Piccolo and Banjo play the night song together now.

If Piccolo sings blowing into his flute:

Merry days are back,

Nights glittering with stars,

Fairies dance and sing,

Clapping their wings.

We are one again, we are again one,

The forest is blessed, the wrong has been undone.

Banjo adds striking his mandolin:

Happy days are back.

All sunny and bright,

Bang bang we party,

All day and night.

Cypher dances to their tunes. Palette had painted almost the whole of the palace tree of the Red Kingdom. All the banished fairies were reunited with their families. Flicker and Scarlet meet at the Great Tree every night and fly down to the Lake of Souls to hear stories from the swans.

Oh, and if you see tiny little light in the forest remember they are not fireflies but lanterns that the fairies hung at their doors on every new moon night.

*** *** *** *** ***

THE IMMORTAL SOUL

The nights had always been cold in this town but that night was arctic. It was the last week of December, seven days to New Year, but still, the temperature was a little too low. The evening had been friendlier with the temperature on the people living in this valley. As the sky grew darker and the night started to grow cold and chilly, the wind began to occupy the streets, replacing the masses. Everybody was hurrying home and I was no exception.

What a night! I thought to myself as I walked against the wind. *It's getting colder by the minute.*

There was no cab running that night.

The wind carried a slight taste of rain in it. I glanced at my watch: 11:30. At my current pace, it would take an hour more to get home. I pulled up the collar of my trench coat and pocketed my hands as it started to rain. The wind died away as soon as the rain started to fall. Now I needed shelter.

The street had few offices and some hotels and restaurants, all closed, but no residences. The recesses of the doors were no match for the heavy torrent. The road had lanes and by-lanes and took any of them as the whim took me in search of a shelter. All the houses were locked and the lights were all out. I was at the end of my wit when I thought I saw a narrow light beaming, and where there is light there is hope. I walked in the direction of the light and came with a small house. It was a double story affair with slanting roofs and a garden currently being washed in the nippy downpour. I opened the small wooden gate and walked to the house.

The house seemed desolate, uninhabited, yet it called to me. Shaking the feeling off my mind, I rang the bell. A few seconds later when the door opened, an elderly lady stood silhouetted in the doorframe.

"Yes?" She asked. There was light in the room behind her. I could not see her face. Her whole being was shrouded in darkness. She appeared to be wearing a knee-long white dress.

I looked at her for a few seconds.

"Yes ma'am," I said quickly. "You see, I am late and I can't get a ride home. It's raining and…"

As though to attest my statement, lightning cracked and thunder rolled cutting me off in the middle of the sentence.

"I understand," she said. "Why don't you come in?"

Inside, the room was warm. I took off my coat and let it hang on the stand.

She had left me alone after closing the door. A few moments later she came out of another room on the opposite side of the hall. The hall was brightly lit and a fire was alight in the fireplace. I wondered why I couldn't see it through the windows. There were a couple of loveseats at the center of the room and a small coffee table in front of them. There were few magazines, one open, and a cup of steaming coffee.

"Here, dry your hair. It is dripping," she said, holding a towel in her outstretched hand. The wrinkles at the corner of eyes deepened when she smiled. I took the towel and rubbed my head while she took a seat on the sofa.

"Thank you very much, ma'am," I said as I sat opposite to her. "I really needed a shelter. It's chilling cold out there."

"What's your name, dear?" She asked. She had a melodious voice.

"I am Judy Dench and I live at Luis Lane."

"I see you work late."

"Got caught up in an emergency."

"Have you had your dinner?"

I stared at her.

"I stay alone here. It won't be a problem if you stay for the night. The storm doesn't seem to go away soon."

At the dining table, we had a chat. Her name was Jeanette Fernandez. It could have been my flattering thoughts but she looked awfully familiar. When I told her so, she just smiled.

A muffled sound woke me up from a sweet dream. I sat up on the bed, searching for the lamp. The room lit up with the small light. It took me a while to get my bearings. Then I remembered that I was in Mrs. Fernandez's house. A glance at my watch told me it was only one in the morning. The storm was still raging outside. I was certain that I had heard something, besides the pouring rain outside but there was no other sound in the house. I turned side and was about to go back to sleep when I heard it again. A gunshot! I jumped off the bed and rushed out of the room.

The house was as still as it had been. Not a soul stirred. Silently I tiptoed my way down the stairs and stood listening to my surroundings. The pitter-patter of the rain continued, the house remained quiet, indifferent.

"Mrs. Fernandez?" I called, uncertainly. No one answered. The door to her bedroom was closed. Taking it to be my imagination, I went back to my room. I stayed awake listening to the falling rain before I finally fell asleep.

Next morning when I went down, I couldn't find Mrs. Fernandez anywhere. I waited for her, looked about the place but there was no sign of her. I was getting late and decided to leave after hurriedly scribbling a note. I thanked her immensely and promised I would visit soon. I put the note on the mantle and left after closing the door behind me.

The morning was really beautiful. After the rain, everything looked fresh and washed. There were no clouds in sight. The roads were busy with people and crammed with vehicles. People were on their way to their jobs; the streets had already started to get crowded. It was much warmer than the night before. I bought a newspaper from the newspaper stand and went to a coffee house and ordered a cup.

While waiting for my coffee I went back to the night before. Was it all a dream or I really did hear a gunshot?

I was woken from my thoughts by the waiter who brought my coffee. I opened the paper and started to read when a column caught my eye. It had a picture of Mrs. Janette Fernandez. The headline said that it was Mrs. Janette Fernandez's 50th death anniversary. She was the greatest actress of her time.

No wonder she looked so familiar, I thought. Then something struck me. I looked at the paper again and re-read the line. It was her 50th death anniversary!

I sprang up from the chair.

It is a hoax, has to be. I mean I just spent the night and…

The way people were staring at me I realized, a little late, that I was talking aloud. Leaving the coffee shop I ran the way I came, pushing away whoever got in the way. I am sure I had turned lots of heads and raised quite a number of eyebrows, but at that time it did not matter.

I was breathing hard when I reached the main door. The house stood in silence just as it was the night before. The garden was laid out quietly.

"Mrs. Fernandez, are you home?" I asked, and waited for an answer. But I did not get one. I called again. Only silence followed.

I ran the lines from the column.

Fifty years ago Mrs. Fernandez was alone in the house.

I pushed the door a little. It was unlocked and opened with a little screech that wasn't there last night. I entered the hall. Sunrays beamed through the windows and lit the dust-filled room. It was deserted.

Fifty years ago it was late at night. There was a storm outside.

The house was perfectly laid out and decorated. Every nook and corner was sheathed with spider web. I went to the adjacent room. She was not there.

Fifty years ago she was. Someone had broken into her house.

I searched the whole house and found no one. On the mantle, I found my note: a new piece of paper among the old.

Fifty years ago she was found in her bedroom, shot through the head.

I left the house just as quiet and calm. Those eyes of hers came back to me time and again, shining like a pair of jewels. My heart thanked her a thousand times and prayed that the immortal soul may rest in peace.

*** *** *** *** ***

MEMORIES ON SALE

The Sunday morning started with a lazy breakfast of cheese sandwiches and apple juice. Then there were the house chores to be done. I looked at my shopping list and sighed. It ran longer than my arm. But my cabinets were nothing more than empty boxes hanging on the walls. So I got up and put on my shoes anyway. A little stroll down to the market wouldn't hurt.

It was around eleven in the morning that I happened to pass by this house of the Morningsides. They are some odd bunch of people in the locality whom most of the neighbourhood tends to avoid. They have peculiar tastes and interests. They have an owl and a raven for pets. Mrs. Summers was saying that day that she had seen an alligator in their swimming pool. They always wear black clothes and you can hear the heavy organ playing in the dead of night. Though they are always smiling and polite, but their neighbours prefer to keep their distance.

As I was walking past their house that morning, Mrs. Morningside came out carrying a box in her hands. When our eyes met, we smiled.

"Good morning, Miss Dench," she said, putting the box down on a table. There were other tables and there were many other boxes too, all scattered over the lawn.

"Good morning, Mrs. Morningside," I nodded. "What's happening here?"

"A garage sale," she said. "Maybe you will find something nice to buy."

I smiled and walked away. I was doubtful that I would find anyone there.

I was returning home with my shopping, about an hour later, when I found a few cars standing in front of the Morningside's place. I was right. There was no one, no one from the neighbourhood, at least. A few unknown faces were wandering about the tables. The Morningsides greeted the customers explaining the great qualities of the items on sale, but no one seemed interested.

Drawn by some unknown curiosity, I stopped to have a look. I put down my bags and went in. All the tables were now occupied by one or other knick-knacks.

On the table to my left was a twelve foot long hosepipe. It was dark green in colour and had been repaired twice. I bent over to have a good look and straightened with a jolt. Both the places had claw marks.

"My Bobby cut it by mistake," John, Mr. Morningside's eight years old son, said. Bobby was a wild, black cat that he had had as a pet. I smiled and went to the next table.

The next table had a wooden box. It was dark brown in colour decorated with copper maple leaves. It looked very pretty. I picked it up and opened the lid. The next moment I dropped it with a shriek. I stood staring at it for a few seconds. Then very carefully I opened it. There was an arm, starting from the elbow till the tip of manicured fingernails. The fingers were long and slender. The arm was thin and fair looking. There were ears fixed on the inside of the lid. They were beautifully curved. My fingers shook as I made to touch it. It was then I realized it that the arm and the ears were artificial.

"That's my grandmother's jewellery box," Liza, Mrs. Morningside's daughter, said. "It's a very original thing. The arm actually belonged to Susie."

I felt a shudder in my bones.

"Susie?" I stammered.

"Yes," she said, shaking her locks. "Susie was the marble statue grandma made. She was a sculptor, you know."

I breathed out in relief and smiled, moving on to the next table.

On that table sat a teapot set. I stopped short at the sight of it. It was black in colour, giving out a magnificent lustre, with golden engravings of poison ivy. The spout of the teapot was curved like a mouth of a snake, its fangs bared and the bifurcated tongue sticking out. The rubies in the eyes were blood red. The handles of the teapot and the cups were shaped like the tails of dragons. It was rather an antique.

"It belonged to my great grandmother," Mrs. Morningside said. "She was quite a snake lover."

I nodded with a smile. It was rumoured that she slept with two snakes with her on her bed and her husband slept in the next room.

I rolled my eyes at the thought, smiled at her and stepped forward.

The next item made me smile. It was not only unique, but the closest thing to normal found on that lawn. It stood six feet above the ground. The wooden body had blackened over the age. The face was yellow with the figures written in big black blocks. The hands were curved and were pointing at five fifty. The glass of the tall case had flowers imprinted on it. The pendulum, with an axe head as its bob, stood silently at the centre of it.

Mr. Morningside came smiling to me.

"Do you wish to buy it, Miss Dench?" he asked.

I shook my head and asked, "Why is the time stopped at five fifty?"

"Oh, that," he said, turning to the clock. "This belonged to my grandfather. It was bought on the day he was born. Not once had it stopped. My grandfather had spent his childhood watching its pendulum swing to and fro. Father said that it chimed uncountable times when granddad brought grandma home for the first time. But it stopped when my grandfather died, at five fifty." He smiled genially. "The clock had never chimed again, but it had kept count of every second of his life."

"A true friend, wasn't it?" I asked. When I turned to him again I found him looking at the clock with tears in his eyes.

As I picked up my bags before leaving, I heard Mr. Morningside telling his son to help him carry the clock back inside. I smiled and unknowingly hummed a tune: My grandfather's clock was too large for the shelf, it la la la…"

*** *** *** *** ***

THE DRAGON'S TALE

Alex breathed in the morning air and exhaled slowly. The cool air made him feel better. He had been burning within for the past thirty years. But it was a price he was willing to pay to protect the forest, his home, and his family. The forest lay like a carpet of green at his feet, treetops swaying with the steady north wind. The creatures were sleeping in their nests, the birds were roosting, the beasts were napping in their dens. There was not a sound, not even a rustle of the leaves. Alex would have heard a twig break. He had the most acute sense of hearing in his clan.

It was his hearing that had saved the *Zeetac* clan that day, so many years ago. He was only seventeen then. Just twelve feet long from head to tail, his black scales had just started to harden, his nails were taking shape, his fangs sharpening. He couldn't breathe fire. None in their clan could, or still can. The best that they could do was to breathe out gray hot smoke. That's why they were such easy preys.

It was near midnight when he heard it. He had crept out of his nest to find some night-berries. They were his favorite and they grew only at night, hence the name. He had loved the night ever since he had cracked out of the egg. In fact, he felt stronger under starlight than he did under the sun.

Very carefully, he crawled out of his nest and came down to the narrow path of the forest. The biggest bush of the night berries was on the western bank of the Great River and he would need to cross the river without being seen by the guards.

They were ever attentive and always ready to strike. They protected the precious *Stone of Power*. It was a gem hidden deep in the forest. Any dragon that could bear the stone would become supreme, but until now no one had the strength to do so. Every dragon that had tried had died.

Alex tiptoed through the forest, keeping himself carefully under the shadows of the night. The smell of the evening flowers intoxicated him. The gentle breeze played lullabies in his ears. He strained his ears, but heard nothing more than the sweet song of the forest fairies.

Alex stopped at the edge of the cliff. This is where he and his brother, Allen, had learned to fly. Their father, Apex, used to push them over the edge when they were only three. The fear of death made them flap their tiny, feeble wings harder. Every time they failed, Apex would carry them up in his claws and push them over. Slowly and steadily, they learned to float and then fly. It not only strengthened their wings, it also made their fear of death disappear. They learned to believe in their wings, in themselves.

Alex looked around for onlookers. In the dark, he could hardly see any. The darkness remained like a solid wall beneath the leaves. Above them the moon shown like a silver medallion. Not that he couldn't see in the dark. He could. They all could. It was one of the Zeetac's specialties. But then there were some who could be almost invisible if desired. They were called the Sheaths. And one of them was Sophie. He scanned the forest as keenly as he could and then stopped. He pricked his ears. He thought he could hear someone breathing. Shaking his head, he spread his wings. Hooking his delicate claws around the edge he posed for flight.

"Boo!"

Alex tumbled over the edge and almost fell over. Somehow managing to claw back to the cliff, he looked up.

"Get down here, Sophie," he growled. "I can hear your wings."

A shadow descended from the sky and came into being. The white scales glittered in the moonlight. She folded her wings making a small cloud of dust float into the air. She had elongated green eyes with the long pupil burning like fire. Alex always thought that she had long eyelashes.

"Out on your night patrol, Alex?" she asked.

"Are you?" Alex questioned. She was about his age. They had learned to fly together. She couldn't breathe fire either, but she wasn't supposed to. She was the one who could go invisible.

"You can't get past the guards, Alex," she said looking over the edge. Two elderly dragons were patrolling the river bed.

"No, but if you make me invisible…" Alex winked and grabbed her arm. "Come on."

Sophie rolled her eyes and stepped forward. She knew how stubborn Alex was.

"Just this one time," she said and peeped over the edge. "On the count of three. Ready?"

Alex didn't answer. He was looking up at the moon.

"Alex," Sophie called. "It's now or never."

Alex was still staring at the sky. It was like he had been turned to stone.

"Last chance, Axe," Sophie chimed. "Or do you want me to tell your…"

Sophie's statement remained unfinished. Alex had jumped on her taking them both down the cliff. They rolled down the slope, their tails, their wings, their long necks tangling and untangling. Accompanying them were chunks of rocks. They stopped on hitting a ledge. Alex freed himself from Sophie and looked up. The place where they were standing had disappeared. Instead, there was a deep groove.

"What was that?" Sophie asked in a whisper. Alex was again looking up at the moon.

This time they both saw it. There was a flash in the sky like lightning and it hit the treetops putting them ablaze. Sophie shrieked as Alex flapped his wings.

"They are coming," he cried. "They are coming for the Stone. You got to warn the guards."

Sophie was shaking in fear. She turned to Alex. "But... But... I can't see them."

"I can hear them," Alex patted her lightly. "Now disappear and warn others. I'll try to lure them away. Go."

As Sophie disappeared into the night, Alex slowly clawed his way up to the top of the cliff. He was right. The Gustaxes were there. He could hear the swing of their wings and the whoosh of their breathing from miles away. They were probably by the southern edge of the forest. One or two had come ahead to gauge the situation.

These Gustaxes had been Zeetac's century long enemies and they had been fighting for ages. They were huge, mean and merciless. Those dragons could breathe fire, and some of them could shoot fiery beams.

They were after the *Stone of Power* and the Zeetacs had been defending the Stone with everything they had, sometimes with their lives. Alex had never really understood why they should always suffer. As he peeped above the edge, he saw two shadows perched on the top of the trees. Straining his ears he could hear more approaching. He only hoped Sophie had alerted the guards and others.

Sophie landed in front of the first guard and came into view. The guard, *Gerald,* looked stunned at first and then frowned.

"Go back to your nest, Sophie," he growled. "Playtime is in the morning."

Sophie, still panting from anxiety, shook her head.

"They are coming," she blurted out. "The Gustaxes are coming."

"Are you sure?"

"Yes… they blew up the cliff top near the western bank. Alex is alone there. They…"

She was interrupted by someone screeching followed by flashes of lightning. Gerald and Sophie looked up to find Alex dashing across the sky, dodging and ducking the lightning. He was flying away from the colony.

"Good boy," Gerald muttered. Turning to Sophie he said, "get back to the colony and wake others up."

Saying so, he flew away to arose the other guards and Sophie disappeared into the night again.

Alex knew his wings weren't strong enough. He was no match for the hundred years old dragons chasing after him. He flapped his wings as hard as he could and went zigzag to confuse his pursuer. He got to do something. Beneath him, he could see the Great River swirling as it went. He could almost touch it. On looking back, he could see the two dragons ready to fire at him. Instantly he folded his wings and dropped straight into the water. The splash drenched the two dragons putting their fire out for a while, giving Alex time enough to escape.

Gerald and other guards were shielding the Stone in every way they could, but this time the Gustaxes appeared stronger. No shields could stand the fiery breath and were melting in an instant. Hurt and injured, Zeetac's dragons retired, replaced by the new ones, but Gerald knew they wouldn't hold for long.

"How are we doing?" Apex asked, landing behind Gerald. *Allen* went out to the defense line with his shield.

Gerald pelted the nearest Gustax with a stone and shook his head. "They are stronger this time. I don't think we can stand longer."

"I'll get the Sheaths," Apex said and flew off.

Sophie woke up everyone in the colony and gathered all the *Sheaths* under the Big Tree. The fire on the western bank created a hellish background. Apex landed in front of them.

"We are under attack," he said in a calm voice. Handling too much of the attack had hardened his nerves. "We'll go with our normal attack mode. But I need two..."

"Sacred chamber breached," one of the guards screamed.

Everyone looked stunned and shocked. Then shock slowly gave way to terror.

"Gather yourselves," Apex yelled. "We still have to save the Stone. Follow me."

The guard's scream was heard far and wide. Alex had heard it too. In fact, he was close enough to see it. A giant of a dragon, encased in golden flames, fell from the sky with tremendous speed, perforating Zeetac's dragon shield and burrowing straight into the sacred chamber. Alex had never seen anything like it before. It was like a hundred times larger than him. The guards fell apart like pieces of twigs in a storm.

Alex flew straight for it. All the guard dragons were lying scattered, burnt and broken. Among them, Alex found his brother, just breathing. Allen would survive, he knew, but seeing his brother lying half dead made his cold blood boil. The Gustaxes were flying in circles above the hole made in the ground. The Giant was at the center of it. Alex knew it would be a disaster if the Giant got hold of the Stone. He had to do something.

It was then he saw Apex, followed by the Sheaths. They fanned out encircling the Gustaxes. Zeetacs couldn't breathe fire. The only defense they had were their sharp nails and the sword that ended their tails. They could cut through rocks. The invisible Sheaths slashed and hacked through the swarm of Gustaxes. They, in turn, blew out flames and lightning beams that took some of the Sheaths unguarded. There were confusion and chaos. Taking advantage of the situation the Giant Gustax broke into the chamber of the Stone. Alex saw him and dived into the hole.

It looked like the earth had been cracked open and a fire was burning inside it. Alex paused at the mouth and shielded his eyes. The Giant was standing in front of the Stone eyeing it with envy.

Alex estimated the Giant was at least a hundred feet long, if not more. He was like a speck of dust in front of him. In the Giant's eye, Alex could see the reflection of the inferno around him. His claws were just above the Stone.

Alex whipped his tail and charged forward. The sword in his tail struck the Giant's hard scale, broke, sending Alex spinning into the ground. Alex shook his head to clear the dizziness. The Giant didn't even feel it. His fingers were closing in on the stone, his lips twisting into an ugly snarl. Alex looked about himself in desperation. There was no one nearby. It was just him and the Giant. Having no other option Alex charged again.

Above the hole in the ground, the Sheaths were in battle with the Gustaxes. It was hard to say who was having an upper hand, but the battle was far from over. Sophie, tearing through the wall of Gustaxes had arrived at the very center of the circle. It was then that her eyes caught the sight. The Giant was reaching for the stone and Alex was dashing for him. Sophie's tail curled in and she bit her nails as she watched Alex shoot towards the Stone. Her eyes went wide with fear as he crashed into the Stone.

There was a blinding explosion blowing up right from the ground, heading skywards, ripping the clouds apart, spreading like a mushroom. When the heat and the light subdued *Sophie* opened her eyes, afraid of what she would see and what she saw made her scales crawl. Most of the dragons were on the ground, lying injured. Gathering some courage she peeped into the hole that looked like a crater of a volcano. Lying like a black stone was the charred body of the Giant Gustax. With a thumping heart, she floated a little further. At the center, where the Stone rested, was now a gaping hole and in that hole was...

" *ALEX* !"

Alex startled and opened his eyes. The grave night of thirty years ago disappeared and a cool dawn with clear blue skies came up.

"Alex," Sophie's voice called again.

He spread his wings and dived for the forest. He was a Giant now, the sole guardian of the Zeetacs. It was a miracle when he survived and gradually the power of the Stone got absorbed into him, giving him enormous strength in his muscles, telescopic eyesight and the power to breathe fire.

As he landed in front of his nest Sophie came running.

"Our first egg is hatching," she spoke excitedly, her green eyes glittering in the morning sun. "Our very first egg."

With his wing around his wife, Alex came inside. Apex and Allen were already there. The brown egg had started to shatter. It cracked and broke into pieces as a little head with big green eyes popped up. Its black scales and the curved nails were yet to form. The little dragon batted its eyes and burped giving out a gust of fire.

*** *** *** *** ***

MAN'S LAST HOPE

Kol stared absently off into the distance, ignoring the bounty before him. Ripe fruits and warm, succulent meats dripped their juices as they hung from the large stake. A roar shook him from his reverie, and he reached over towards Chiara, stroking her smooth dragon scales. "Yes, I know, girl. The sky traders are coming. I'm just as excited to meet her."

Chiara responded by sticking the tip of her nose under his shoulder and pushing him toward the saddle.

Kol caressed his dragon a little and put his foot in the stirrup. He was about to press himself up when his communicator in his ear beeped. Two small ones and one long one. Dola. She was arriving tonight. They had only spoken over the video confab. It was the first time that they would meet.

He activated the link.

"Hey, Dola." He smiled, remembering her doll-like face. "How far…"

"Help!" Dola's voice came in a whisper. "We… we… we are attacked." She spoke in between breaths.

Kol looked up at the sky. Those tiny dots were the vessels from Earth carrying the last band of the Earthlings.

"You are about to enter our atmosphere," Kol argued.

"Santurns." Dola kept her voice low. "They have taken over, imprisoned us. Don't be deceived."

"But…"

"Inform the stations. Don't let…ah!" Dola's voice broke off in a scream of anguish. Kol tore the communicator from his ear. It hurt, both ways.

Kol looked up at the sky once more. The Earth had been in trade with the Uranions for centuries. As the conditions on that planet declined, it became necessary for them to import food from out of space. So when the live-giving Sun started to die, it threatened to char the planet after devouring Mercury and Venus. The sun had turned into a Red Star, killing most of the life on Earth. Humans were already an endangered species by then. Uranus offered home which the Earth gladly accepted.

*** *** ***

It was not a hand but a paw. The fingers were like hotdog buns and the nails sharp and bent like an eagle. The man, if she could call him that, was ten feet tall. His chest looked like a nose of a truck with arms like a limb of a crane. And to her horror, he had four of those. The face was black with a pair of red orbs for eyes and a crack for lips. There was no nose, just nostrils above the lips.

Dola had only heard about these Santurns but seeing them so close crushed her heart. The fingers were clasped around her neck. He was speaking over his communicator. His other three hands had weapons Dola had never seen.

These Santurns, the hideous beasts from Saturn, were the Uranions' ancient enemies. They had been trying to take over Uranus because of the bountiful nature of the planet. So far they had been defeated by the Uranion army. An army that sored heights and could breathe helium without a hitch, had telescopic vision, were precious. A species that could breed massive beasts called dragons and fire-breathing dragons at that, would be priceless.

"Ya," the Santurn said and turned to Dola. She shrunk under his gaze. "You, Earthling. Who you call?"

"No… no one," she stammered. "No link."

A small pen like thing jabbed the side of her torso making her scream. Bolts of electricity ran through her body, tingling through the bones.

"Who you call? Uranions?"

Dola coughed, tasting blood in her mouth, and clawed the rocky hand to free her neck but her strength had abandoned her. Trying hard to keep her eyes open she continued to gasp for breath.

The Santurns had captured and overpowered their fifteen ships. They had no defense to stop the Santurns. The Uranions were expecting friends. They would immediately recognize these to be the sky traders and let them through. The Santurns were counting on the surprise element and if that failed, they would use the humans as shields. There's no telling what havoc they would unleash over the unsuspecting Uranions. Did she get her message through? Did Kol understand her? Could he inform the army in time? He better. Thirty thousand Earthmen were depending on it. The last of all mankind.

*** *** ***

Chiara tore through the sky, the clouds, the wind, covering miles with one flap of her leathery wings. Kol held on with both his hands, head buried in her neck. Cool air rippled through his clothes, yet he felt sweat on his forehead.

Dola's words rang in his ears. 'Santurns' she had whispered, 'they had taken over.'

The chill ran down his spines over and over again at the mere thought of what the beasts did to the humans who were nothing more than mere flies to them. His body gave an involuntary shiver to think of the torture that Dola would need to endure. She was caught, Kol knew. Would he see her alive, he doubted.

Wiping the tears he didn't know an Uranion was capable of shading, he urged Chiara to fly faster. The dragon bellowed and forced herself further.

He tried his communicator to reach his father, Hal, time and again but he found the link busy. Well, fifteen ships carrying thirty thousand Earthlings were almost ready to touchdown. The commander of the Army would be busy. Kol tried another link.

"This is Lola," a female voice said. "Officer in charge at station four."

"I know who you are, sister," Kol said. "Now listen very carefully. The… Santurns… have… taken… over… the… Earth… vessels." The wind snatched words from his lips flying them away. He just hoped that Lola had been able to hear and comprehend.

There was an unending silence of five seconds.

"Meet me and father at station five." The link disconnected.

*** *** ***

In a cold corner of a hold, Dola crouched and shivered. Lips torn and bleeding and bruises and cuts all over her face, she waited for her agony to end. Her dress was soaked in blood and so was her hair. She had heard Kol's voice for the last time. She wished she could see him, feel him before she died. But it is a lost dream now. If Kol had understood her then their ships would be blown out of existence before they entered the atmosphere. The Uranions would never risk an invasion for the sake of an endangered species, that too from another planet. She sighed letting the pain take over her and closed her eyes, oblivious of the vibration in the ship, the friction on the hull or the fire cone that covered the tip of the vessel as it plunged into the thermosphere.

*** *** ***

Commander Hal listened to his daughter and looked up at the sky.

"Father," Lola said. "We must stop them."

Hal nodded. His brows were still knotted tight.

"Father. We must destroy the ships."

"No Lola." Hal's calm voice almost touched Lola. "I gave the Earthlings hope. I'm not going to shatter them with my own hands."

"But the Santurns would just torture them and use them as a shield. They might try and barter the lives of the humans for Uranus."

"I understand." Hal turned and put a hand on Lola's shoulder. "Ready every man on duty. Call back those on leave. Gear up the dragons. Gather every weapon. We congregate at the landing site. Go."

With her orders clear, Lola scuttled to fulfill them, hoping against hope that things would pull off. Or else two worlds would perish in the fire.

*** *** ***

Chiara stopped all of a sudden almost throwing Kol off her back.

"What is it, girl?" He asked passing his hand over her silver scales. She started going in circles. Chiara raised her head and roared.

Kol followed her gaze and found blazing stars in the sky.

"Blessing Oberon! They have entered the atmosphere," he mumbled.

"Kol," Hal's voice cracked through his communicator. "Meet us at the landing site."

Before Kol could reply the link was gone.

"Towards the landing site, Chi," he patted her and she rolled and disappeared under the clouds.

*** *** ***

Quarm, the Santurn lord, stood behind the pilot and watched as the vessel carefully hovered over the landing pad. Through the windscreen, he could see about twenty Uranion army-men standing in a semicircle with Hal at the center. The grip around his trident tightened and lips stretched in a sneer. His plan had worked. The Uranions didn't suspect a thing. The army commander appeared unarmed.

The vessel settled on the pad like a feather landing on water. The hatchway opened with a hiss.

Outside the Uranions waited in frozen anticipation. Hal stood facing the fifteen ships standing in three neat rows. The hatchways yawned.

Hal's fist tightened.

One by one the Earthlings started to descend. Children, men, women, old and young. They huddled together looking uncertain. Those scared and tearstained faces told their tale.

Hal ground his teeth and watched the hatchway.

At first, there was no movement. Then all of a sudden a loud yell came from inside. Feet clambered and tall and wide figures of Santurns came flowing out of the hatchway carrying deadly weapons in four hands. They took places in between the groups of Earthlings. Last came Quarm.

Seeing the Army weaponless Quarm smiled in satisfaction.

"Now you surrender," he spoke to Hal. "Or we kill humans."

Hal eyed him for a while and nodded lightly.

"Men," he said quietly. "Destroy them."

Quarm got time enough to widen his eyes before streams of fire rained on them. Dragons, black, red, grey and silver that had remained hidden rose and breathed on them. A few flew over them picking them up and dropping them from heights. Army-men swarm in from all sides with swords and shields.

The Earthlings screamed in fear, men protecting the women, the women protecting the children. Minutes later they realized that the fire didn't reach them in any way. They were quite safe in an invisible enclosure that shielded them from the fire and Santurns' weapons.

Quarm bellowed in anger as his men burned and charred in front of him.

He drew his trident and jumped for Hal. Hal stepped back but a sword swung chopping Quarm's top right arm. Quarm screamed and turned to find Lola with her sword dripping his inky blood.

From above Kol could see the crossfire at the landing site. Chiara, retracting her wings, nosedived zeroing in on the battlefield. Kol scanned the human groups for Dola but he couldn't see her. Just above the field, Chiara pulled up breathing over the Santurns who defied the other dragon's fire. Her breath stunned them, freezing them in place. The army-men cut them into pieces. Inside an hour the landing pad was covered in the red blood of the Uranions and the black blood of the Santurns.

The field was littered with scorched bodies, severed limbs, and heads. Quarm stood alone in the field. After losing two of his top hands he looked smaller. Lola stood posed with her sword. Chopping Quarm's arms had given her great pleasure.

"I come back," Quarm threatened but sounded hollow. He knew there was no coming back. He didn't have a single man alive. The army-men tightened the circle around him.

Hal extended his hand. Lola gave up her sword.

"You are a threat not to my people alone, but to all sentient being existing in the universe. I, the commander of Uranion Army and the master of Uranus, would do what should be done. But before that I would give you a chance. Surrender and live."

Quarm spat.

"I not scared." He growled and then sprang upon Hal. The commander took a step back and drove the sword into Quarm's chest piercing his all three hearts at once.

The battle over, the Uranions ushered the Earthlings towards their villages. Chiara landed and Kol leaped off her back.

One after the other he combed the vessels in search of Dola. He couldn't even pick up her heat signature. Fourteen ships had turned him down. With his heart thudding in his ears he stepped into the fifteenth vessel. After scrutinizing whole of it, he came to the hold. In a cold corner, covered in blood was lying a girl. There was no movement in her. Kol cuddled her in his arms. With trembling fingers, he held her wrist. More imagined than felt, he could sense the faint beating of her pulse.

*** *** *** *** ***